Suddenly Rico yanked his fishing rod and grunted with excitement. Something was biting! "Nice and easy," instructed Skipper. "Remember: The toppings are more scared of you than you are of them."

"Whoa, big fella!" Skipper cried as his fishing line tugged him forward. The hot dog man pushed his cart away . . . and pulled Skipper right off the branch!

"Ow! Oomph! Eek!" Skipper yelled as he hit branch after branch on the way down to the ground.

I WAS A PENGUIN ZOMBIE!

by Molly Reisner

Grosset & Dunlap
An Imprint of Penguin Group (USA) Inc.

© 2011 Viacom International Inc. Madagascar ® DWA L.L.C. All Rights Reserved. Used under license by Penguin Young Readers Group. Published by Grosset & Dunlap, a division of Penguin Young Readers Group, 345 Hudson Street, New York, New York 10014. GROSSET & DUNLAP is a trademark of Penguin Group (USA) Inc. Printed in the U.S.A.

ISBN 978-0-448-45619-5   10 9 8 7 6 5 4 3 2 1

One afternoon at the New York Zoo, the Penguins began their latest mission: Operation Fish Picnic. Perched high up in a tree, they fished for tasty fish toppings from the hot dog man's cart. With ketchup and mustard, their fish would be even more delicious!

THWOMP! Skipper face-planted right into the grass!
The Penguins slid down the tree trunk to check on their leader.

Kowalski saw that something was terribly, horribly wrong! "Broken, broken, broken!" he sputtered, pointing to Skipper. Rico and Private shuddered when they caught sight of Skipper's crumpled-up wing.

"You need to see the doctor!" ordered Kowalski.

"No, thanks, amigo. And besides, maybe I'm double-jointed," he said, batting his wonky wing around. It hurt to move, but Skipper refused to admit he was injured.

"Great! Then we can still play volleyball!" cheered Private.

During volleyball, Skipper stifled his moans as he hit the ball with his bad wing. No way was he going to the doctor!

"Double! Jointed!" Skipper explained through gritted teeth.

"Great! Then we can still arm-wrestle!" said Private.

Over in the elephant habitat, Skipper and Burt faced off in a round of arm wrestling. Burt snaked his trunk around Skipper's broken wing and easily pinned it down. "*Gah!* You didn't even use an arm!" Skipper cried.

Kowalski noticed Skipper's wing was throbbing. "Is your double-jointed wing turning a little swollen-y?" he asked.

"It's nothing!" Skipper squeaked.

Private clapped. "Great! Then we can still go to high-five practice!"

Rico high-fived Skipper's wing . . . right to the ground!
"Aaargh!" Skipper hollered, falling backward.
"I guess that's why we need practice," said Private.

At that moment, Alice the zookeeper walked by and snatched up Skipper. "Look at your wing! That's got to be infected!" she said.

The Penguins exchanged concerned looks. "Infected . . . ?" gasped Private as Alice hurried off with Skipper in her arms.

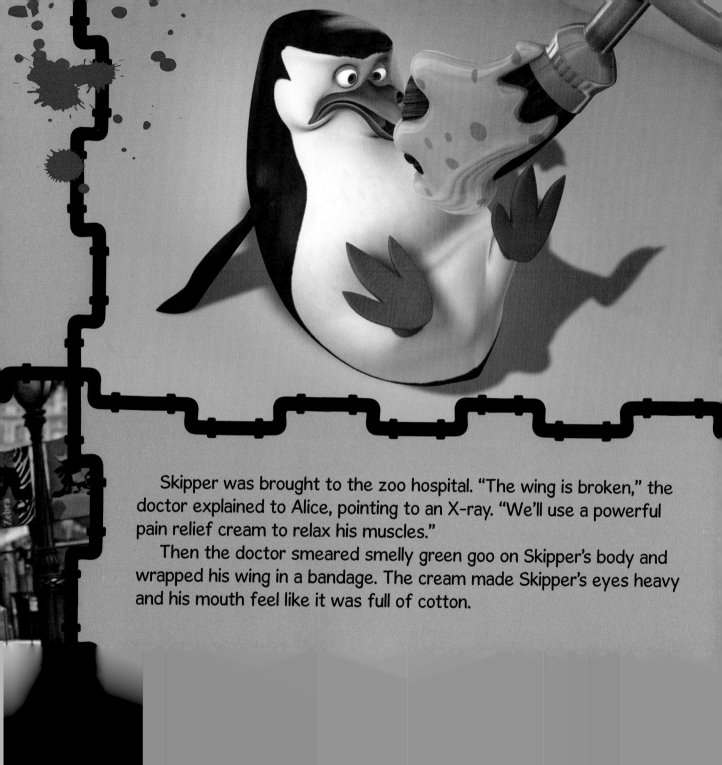

Skipper was brought to the zoo hospital. "The wing is broken," the doctor explained to Alice, pointing to an X-ray. "We'll use a powerful pain relief cream to relax his muscles."

Then the doctor smeared smelly green goo on Skipper's body and wrapped his wing in a bandage. The cream made Skipper's eyes heavy and his mouth feel like it was full of cotton.

"I'll keep him here for a few days, but he'll be fine," the vet said, placing Skipper in a cage. When the people left, Skipper hauled himself upright. He was in a deep daze from the medicine and everything was blurry. But he was determined to escape!

Skipper managed to open the cage, then aimed a roll of bandages toward the window. He wanted the roll to unravel so he could climb up it like a rope and escape to freedom. *BAM!* It hit the TV power button instead.

A show came on the screen. "Doctor! Did we operate in time?" asked the actress.

"There's always time . . . for love," said the actor.

Skipper threw the bandages again. "Gaggahaaba!" he shouted excitedly. It worked!

Meanwhile, Skipper's buddies snuck up to the hospital wall and formed a penguin ladder. "Private, describe to us what you see," commanded Kowalski.

"Wall, possibly brick," said Private. They were one penguin short of being able to see inside Skipper's window.

Voices from the silly doctor show wafted out the window.
"The infection in the brain has done horrible things! There's nothing we can do. It's over," Private heard the TV doctor say. The Penguins were worried. They had no idea it was just the people on TV talking!

Back inside Penguin Headquarters, the three friends huddled together. "Skipper's . . . gone? What'll we do?" said Private.

Kowalski put on a brave face. "We'll soldier on like men!" he said. Then he and Private immediately started bawling uncontrollably. Rico coughed up a picture of Skipper and hugged it tightly.

Meanwhile, Skipper escaped from the hospital to find his friends. But not without accidentally wrapping himself in bandages and rolling around in baby powder first! Exhausted, he dragged one foot behind him with each step. Under the glow of the full moon, Skipper looked 100 percent ghoulish.

A raging storm shut down all the lights. Unable to see, Skipper fell into the penguin habitat. "Hagablaaaag," he howled upon landing. Kowalski turned on a flashlight. "It's Skipper!" Private exclaimed. "That's not him anymore," Kowalski whispered. "You heard the doctor. That infection did things to his brain. I'd say . . . *zombie* things."

Skipper lumbered toward the Penguins. "Guahaabaa?" he said, spooking everyone.

"Is he dangerous?" asked Private.

Always prepared, Kowalski gave out helmets. "You bet your brain he is. Protect your heads. And move slowly toward the—" began Kowalski, trying not to panic.

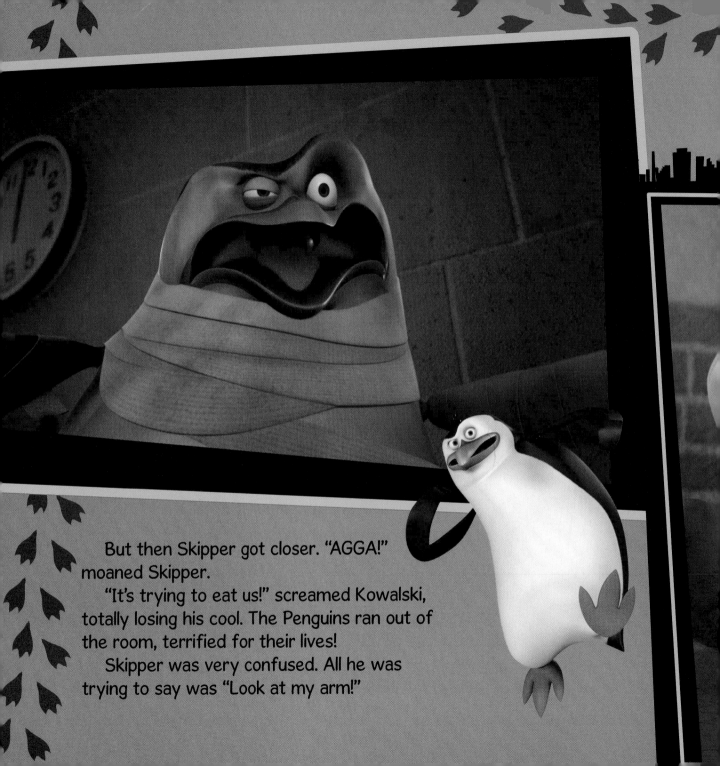

But then Skipper got closer. "AGGA!" moaned Skipper.

"It's trying to eat us!" screamed Kowalski, totally losing his cool. The Penguins ran out of the room, terrified for their lives!

Skipper was very confused. All he was trying to say was "Look at my arm!"

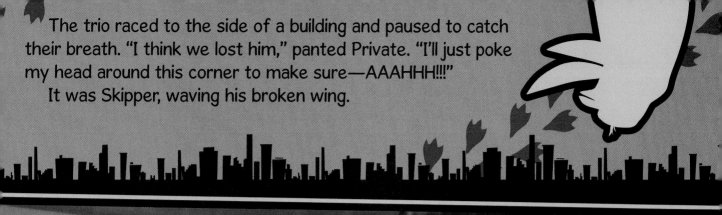

The trio raced to the side of a building and paused to catch their breath. "I think we lost him," panted Private. "I'll just poke my head around this corner to make sure—AAAHHH!!!"

It was Skipper, waving his broken wing.

Nowhere was safe from the dreaded Skipper-like creature! "The best place to hide from zombies is in a small, dark room with creepy lighting," said Kowalski as the Penguins huddled inside the reptile house.

Just then, Skipper slammed into a nearby window. "Garburglehaaba!" he screeched.

"Perhaps I'm wrong!" yelled Kowalski. They ran as fast as they could.

Next, the Penguins crammed themselves inside a trash can. Kowalski monitored the area with binoculars. "Is he gone?" whispered Private.

Kowalski nodded his head. Then he said, "All clear!"

A second later, Skipper popped up from behind the trash can. "Hagaburgleflug!"

He teetered on the edge of the can and soon lost his balance. *SLAM!* Everyone went flying to the ground.

Skipper caught up with his fleeing friends at the zoo café. "Can we help him?" said Private. He missed Skipper—even if he had become a monster.

Kowalski came up with a brilliant plan. "If we capture Skipper, we can find a cure for his zombie-ism! Of course, we'd have to conduct a series of tests first . . ."

Zombie? Tests? Skipper spun around, catching a reflection of himself in the café window. Holy bandaged beast! He *did* look like a zombie! Now if he could just convince his friends of the truth . . .

But it was too late! The Penguins chased Skipper up to a rooftop. "Remember, zombies can't feel a thing. No mercy this time, boys!" yelled Kowalski.

Rico concentrated hard and spit up a chain saw. *Uh-oh.* Skipper was surrounded!

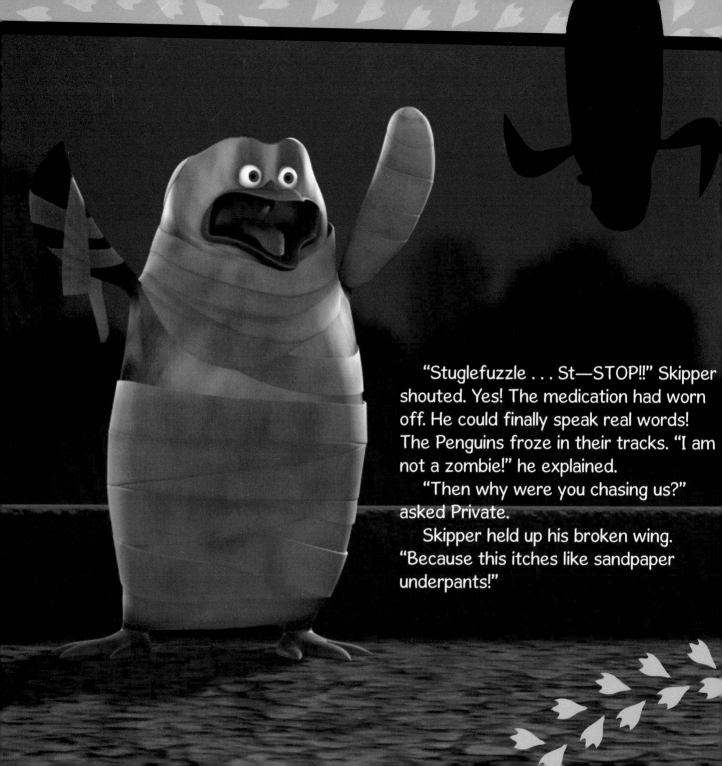

"Stuglefuzzle . . . St—STOP!!" Skipper shouted. Yes! The medication had worn off. He could finally speak real words! The Penguins froze in their tracks. "I am not a zombie!" he explained.

"Then why were you chasing us?" asked Private.

Skipper held up his broken wing. "Because this itches like sandpaper underpants!"

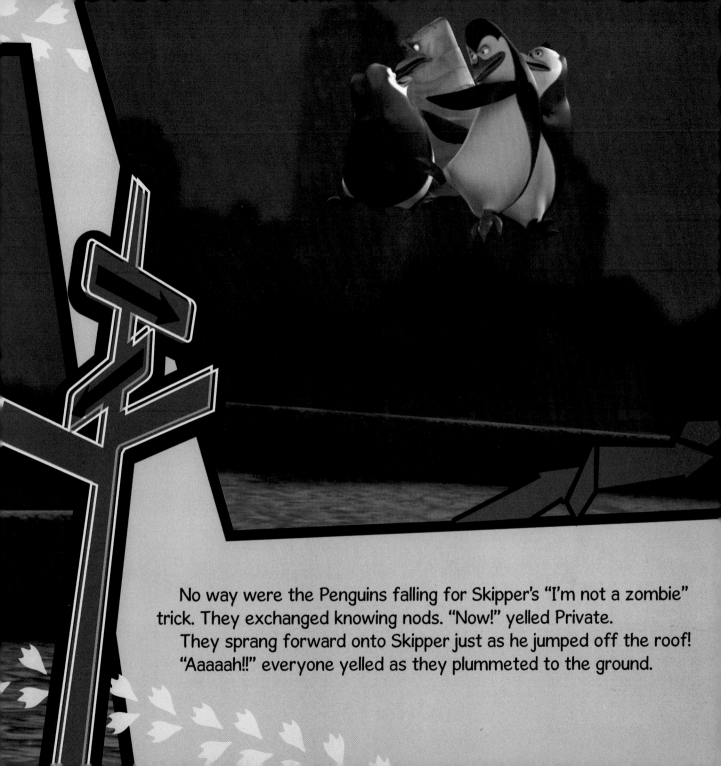

No way were the Penguins falling for Skipper's "I'm not a zombie"
trick. They exchanged knowing nods. "Now!" yelled Private.
    They sprang forward onto Skipper just as he jumped off the roof!
"Aaaaah!!" everyone yelled as they plummeted to the ground.

The Penguins ended up in the hospital with broken wings and were sleepy from the pain-relieving cream.

"See, I told you I wasn't a zombie," Skipper said to his bandaged buddies.

Rico, Kowalski, and Private could only say one thing back: "Garbleflagglehaaga!"